Charlie Bonker 3

All the way from Pottage Pie

Memories and Moments

www.BonkerBooks.com

For the preservation of world wildlife

Characters

Charlie Bonker: Top Feral cat

Indy: One eyed Feral

Gigs: Tomboy tortoiseshell

Balloo: A boring black cat

Poo: The Staffie

Vermin Pork belly: The rat

Trike: A disabled dog

Mackison: A stuck up Persian cat

Purditta: A posh Persian cat

Charlie had sulked underneath the stairs for just over a week. The computer hadn't been as helpful as he'd hoped, the flights were more than he'd imagined, and credit cards were something that, Charlie'd never heard of. Then out of the blue, Becky makes an astonishing announcement.

Chapter

Charlie had come to realize that there were many moments in life, some worth keeping, others, damn well trying, like the day the computer asked for a credit card. The company was called Speedy Jet, but as Charlie found out, they were anything but fast! Furious, Charlie abandoned the page and left the computer. Spain appealed to Becky far more than the house Denis wanted in Devon. Why move into a centrally heated house with a courtyard, when they could have sun and sand? All she had to do, was convince Denis.

Credit Card and Cargo

"The cats are nothing but an inconvenience! I'm not paying out hundreds for them!" Opposed to the idea of wasting cash on Becky's cats, Denis complained bitterly.

"Well, we can't leave them behind they're family!"

"To you maybe…! What have they ever done for me?"

"Tit for tat, that's all it ever is with you. Why can't you accept them like we do your Trike?"

"Trike is a good dog, not a dirty dustbin hunter like your cats!"

Disappointed with the way the conversation was going, Charlie stopped spying on them and made his way into the garden towards Gigs.

"Gosh, I hate him!" Upset by the decision Charlie's legs gave way.

"He's always been tight," Gigs replied, "and let's face it, he'd rather drink himself senseless than save us."

"He's a nerd," Charlie huffed, "a nasty nincompoop!"

"Don't worry," Balloo scrambled out of the house, "Becky has refused to go without us. And guess what…?

"Don't tell me," Charlie pulled a crude face, "nasty nerd has withdrawn his no?"

"Oh, belt up Charlie," said, Poo, "think yourself lucky you've even got a ticket. Most owners would have left you outside the cat pound and kept their cash."

"That may be so, but I have Becky," Charlie wasn't in a pleasant mood. "Think yourself lucky you, haven't been left to the butcher."

"What dya mean you feather brain feline…!" Poo retaliated.

"According to customs, crabby, the cost reflects the weight of the individual."

"So," said, Poo.

"Well, you'll break the bank and the travel box, won't you?"

"Stop it," Trike, was unsure of it all, "what about the wildlife we've befriended? You like Vermin, don't you?" Trike eyed the garden for him.

"Of course, I like Vermin," Charlie placated, "but he is exactly that, wild. Whereas you my friend are fed and watered, like every other domestic dog."

"Huh, I wish!"

"Just because your disabled, doesn't mean you can't do stuff!"

"Are you for real Charlie, feel that stump!" Born a cripple, Trike pushed his left shoulder forward. Nothing but bone, skin covered

the stump where his leg had not grown.

"You're a wobbling whiner," Charlie joked, "you've got three other legs that still work, and a front wheel, haven't you?"

Before Trike could return the banter, Becky entered the garden and positioned herself beside Poo, who was in deep dog thought. Raising her arms, Becky called for their attentions.

"Now, I know none of you really understand me, but I want to tell you anyway."

"Were not stupid, we already know about Spain and all that stuff. So there, who, doesn't understand?" Charlie said while sucking up to her and making sure that his tail stroked her chin every few seconds.

"Well," Becky continued, "were going to live somewhere sunnier, and guess what?" Scooping Charlie up, Becky held him before her face. "Indy's owners rang to say he hadn't been the same since Samba's death. They asked if we wanted him, and guess what, packed and prepared, he arrives tomorrow." She put Charlie down.

The animals let out a sigh of satisfaction. Becky returned to the house to try and comfort a very disgruntled Denis. Change wasn't something he liked, especially when it was costing money, an extra cat too...

"Don't be so sad," said Becky, "you'll be doing a lot of good giving the animals a broader life."

"It would be cheaper if they just all got lost!"

"You don't mean that. I think you'd miss them if they weren't here."

"Yeah, right, I'd rather a barrel of beer than that furry lot any day."

"You would, wouldn't you?" Becky appeared concerned. "What about the hens?"

"Old boilers have had it. Not fit for the fox!"

"Ooh, chicken soup at last." Ear wigging as usual, it was Charlie.

"I'll ask Maud if she will have them." Becky left and headed to the manor where she negotiated a new hen home.

After weeks of organization the dogs and cats were put into cages and carried to the car. Trike's wheel dismantled, he was put into an even larger cage and slid beside the cats.

"This is a joke right!" Charlie sneered from behind the plastic bars. "Becky's, having a laugh, isn't she?" He glanced at Trike who, without his wheel support, had fallen to one side.

"A little discomfort," Trike droned, "could turn into a dream."

"Oh, shut up, you lopsided lunatic!" Charlie sneered.

Passports in her bag, Becky smiled one last time at the old house, slammed the boot, and nodded for Denis to start the car. At the airport they met a woman who handed over a cage. Inside it, was Indy. Unlike Charlie, who had shut his feelings away, Indy, was still visibly depressed over Samba. Sad, he pulled his patch further over his eye and hid under his blanket. Two security guards with funny sideburns and short shaven chins approached.

"You must be Denis and Becky?" The voice was deep. "Don't worry we'll take good care of them."

"Do what you like with them," Den, hissed under his breath, "just not the dogs."

The animals were stacked onto a trolley and wheeled away. Looking behind, they watched an apprehensive Becky, and delighted Den, disappear.

"Little Denis," sniggered Charlie, "getting smaller and smaller by the minute."

"Do you know how much this trip has actually cost?" Balloo defended Denis.

"Don't know, don't care. How's that." Charlie was lifted off the trolley, and placed on a rickety conveyer belt, "hang on," he screeched, "what's this?" Disappearing towards the dark hold Charlie didn't like it. "What happened to first class flying, fluffy cushions, fine foods and fresh milk?"

"I guess, they heard you were coming." Trike teased.

Reaching the baggage handlers, the cages were removed, rowed up and secured to the wall. The animals were given a blanket and only an inch of water in case of spillages. Wedged between Indy and

5

Balloo, Charlie took a good look around. "It's a space ship, a severely, cold one at that."

"What, if they're sending us to the moon?" It was Poo.

"Don't worry, you'll crash back to earth pretty quick."

"How so…?" Poo glared for Charlie to finish.

"Cos you're too fat to float or free fall."

Charlie was still chuckling when checked in luggage was securely stacked higher than the eye could see.

"I'm glad we don't have to carry cases around!" Poo pouted.

"You are a case!" Charlie glared at her, "a nut, case."

A loud speaker broke up the banter and made them jump. "This is your Captain speaking please fasten your seat belts."

"All we've got is a squelchy moth ridden box! Shows how much they care about our safety." Charlie, clung to the bars, fears hidden, he frothed some more. "I hate humans, for their selfishness. It should be us sat up there, and all of them, cramped down here. I mean, heck, what do they think we're gonna do?"

"Be sick on them or do a number two!" Balloo burst into a babble of laughter.

The aircraft door closed, and suddenly, they were engulfed in darkness. Startled, the cats sat upright, their shiny eyes examining their dismal surroundings in the process. The sound of tiny feet pattering on the tacky tin floor, gave them all cause for concern.

"It's a ghost," cried Gigs, "something sent by Den, to eat us."

6

"Lost in transit." Charlie snuffled, "suit, him wouldn't it?"

"No, it's not," said Indy, "it's something much smarter!" Indy didn't know how he knew, he just did. The rattling of a box was heard, one strike and the place lit up. Holding up a candle it was Vermin. A smile reaching from one ear to the other, a grimace decorated his grey face.

"I knew it was you," said Indy, "you have a distinct smell about you."

"I'll take that as a compliment, shall I?" Vermin held the candle higher to see him clearly.

"So, what's going on?" Indy insisted. "How come you came?"

"You didn't think, I was gonna miss paella, peanuts, and sangria, did you?" He glanced at Charlie, "wild, I'll give you wild, were going to have a wicked time."

A second later they felt the plane begin to move. Slowly at first, but then gathering momentum it got faster and faster until it began to tilt one end, forcing Vermin to slide down the middle of it. The candle went out and the aircraft left the ground. In total darkness, the animals held their breath as the metal bird sailed into the sky. Charlie felt his stomach begin to shrink; then sucked away by an invisible vacuum, he felt very sick, ears popping, he thought his head was going to explode. Terrified by the take-off, Charlie couldn't speak, his mouth was moving, but the words were not coming out. Then, eventually, a faint sound emerged…

"Vermin are you alright?" The weakened words of Charlie wafted towards the end of the plane. There was no reply. Charlie began to fret and pine for home. Gravity still pulling he cried out.

7

"The best place in the world was my bed, I was always happy in my bed."

"That's just depressing," it was Trike.

"No, it's not," Charlie whimpered, "it's warm!"

"Think yourself lucky you weren't left behind."

Just then the plane reached its altitude straightening the hold accordingly. Another candle lit, and Vermin breathed a sigh of relief, clambering up from the exit doors he stood once again in front of them all.

"Well," he puffed, "that was just horrible!"

"Big time." Charlie complained, "my back is killing me!"

"That's what happens when you've got no brain cells to hold you up." Poo cackled at him.

"Well," Charlie confirmed, "it's one more than you've got!"

Putting the candle down and taking a hair pin from his dungarees, Vermin picked the lock on Poo's cage, pulling the handle he let her out. Vermin then proceeded to open the other cages. Free in the hold the animals searched for something to eat and drink. Opening the first of many cases, Gig's found nothing but clothes. Stuffing them back, she watched Charlie rummage through a second case.

"Bingo." He beamed. A box of Belgium chocolates in one hand he held a bottle of Baileys in the other. "I've heard it's a clotted kind of cream."

Charlie unscrewed the lid and broke one of the chocolates into several sections.

"They reckon chocolate can kill dogs." Poo was hesitant.

"Best you don't have any then." Charlie took a big bite of his and teased her.

Tipsy on Baileys, their travel fears were soon forgotten. The cats made so much fun of the humans that they didn't even feel the turbulence. Turbulence, that made everyone above them blush and belch. Two hours later exhausted and excited, they felt the pull of gravity. Going down they got ready to land.

Putting the empty bottle back, Charlie sniggered, "it's great to think that some human will be blamed for this." Closing the empty chocolate box, Charlie slid it back into the case. "Vermin," he yelled, "get in here otherwise we might lose you on landing." Charlie held his blanket open. Warm and inviting Vermin brushed against him. "Just don't get too close, you hear me!"

Ears ringing, the animals tried to ignore the pain. As they got closer to the ground they felt as if they had been wrung out. A loud thud, and they were skimming the runway, wheels grinding they came to a halt. It felt good to be back on the ground where nature intended them to be. Departing the aircraft, sunshine, put, a smile on their faces. Yes, the animals were ready for Spain!

Pedigrees and the Peasant

The rented house was a typical two-bedroomed, Spanish semi. Small outside but evidently, enormous inside. Terracotta floor tiles enhanced its grey walls, broken sink and shower. Very basic the house contained only cane furniture that extended itself into a utility room. There, Becky released the cats and tried to make them feel at home.

"Seven days that's all." Busy filling food and water bowls, Becky, didn't notice Vermin. "In here you stay, that way you won't stray." Becky filled some trays with small stones and shut them all in.

"What a load of litter tray trash!" Charlie said eyeing the windowsill. "I'm off gallivanting until my guts groan for grub. I'll be back then." Leaping and teetering, onto the window ledge, he leaned his weight on its frame till it opened.

"Be careful Charlie," Vermin cringed, "there are some heavy, feral out there!"

"How the bells would you know?" Charlie clapped both paws on his chin and peered down at him for an answer.

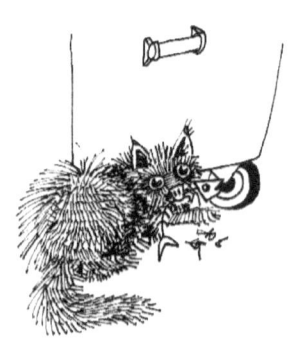

"I saw them scattered around when we stopped."

"My parents were feral!" Charlie squeezed through the gap.

"Wait for us!" Gigs, Balloo and Indy followed him onto a dividing wall. Built on a lower level, next door, was a long way down. Scurrying along its top, Balloo, lost her balance and fell some twenty feet. There, unhurt, she was trapped in a square courtyard.

"Stay there," shouted, Gigs, "we will look for a rope!"

"She's hardly going, anywhere is she?" Charlie couldn't help himself.

The cats continued along the wall to its end. A mountain forest ran alongside the houses, branching off near a large car park. Paramount, the view was priceless.

. "Wow," Charlie purred, "a model village made especially for me."

"You wish..." Indy brushed past his brother and dropped down onto the village road. Frowned upon as intruders, they immediately felt intimidated. From under cars, trees and bench tops, balconies and bars, the cats felt a cold intense chill from the onlookers.

"Stay cool," said Charlie, "they may be wild, but we're from the west."

"You don't narf ramble some rubbish at times, don't you?" Indy straightened his eye patch and chuckled.

Together, the cats wandered cautiously up the hill. Passing a bar, they paused. There, hovering in a corner, a tiny feral cried for scraps. Suddenly the bar door swung open, a second later a shower of water soaked the kitten.

"Hey," said a tabby feral, "there's no need for that, he's only a midget."

11

"Then send him down the shallow end of town," a brown domesticated cat sucked up to its owner, "the little runt is making a nuisance of itself. Go on, get your own food."

"Just wait till you have to fend for yourself!" Calling to the kitten, the tabby took off with it in tow.

Charlie and his crew continued to a large green garbage bin in a car park. There, looking more like a balloon than a black cat was sat a pedigree Persian. The cat displayed despicable cheek. One that made even Charlie question the very existence of such a spoilt, overweight, sack of stuffed skin. The Persian put aside a bone it was sucking on and put a greasy paw out to greet him.

"Mackison is the name, freedoms the game..."

"Well," said Charlie, "by the size of you, there can't be much game left in the valley."

Mackison was unimpressed and made a loud snuffling sound that everyone found somewhat embarrassing.

"If I had a laugh like that," Charlie mocked, "I'd think twice before entering a public place."

"Perhaps..." Mackison straightened up, "you should consider your own personal predicament. I mean this is my car park, not yours."

On its outskirts gathered feral cats. Obstinate eyes all around them, Charlie and the cats suddenly felt unsafe.

"It's, ok lads," Mackison confirmed, "they're with me!"

Mackison looked at Charlie in particular. "You have to be seen to be with authority, otherwise, they will tear you up and run your torn fur out of town."

"What gives an arrogant snob like you that sort of clout?"

"My Persian blood and food my friend, food…!" Mackison rubbed his stomach and belched a deep bellied laugh.

"Where," mumbled Gig's, "would you get enough food from?"

"My overweight owners…" Mackison pointed up at a balcony where they were both sat. "He's Gin and she's tonic," he laughed. "Not really its Miguel and Mandy, while he boozes, she spends her time buying expensive foods. Foods that I can't stand. It does however give me a lot of shout in the village. I love their scraps, and they love my silly science diet, giving me the authority to do as I please without any comebacks."

"And the other…?" Charlie referred to the man. "He looks rather sour."

"That's because amongst being sad and stupid, he is. I mean let's be honest, what sort of man prefers a cat to a dog, especially a Persian. It, kind of desecrates the saying, A Dog's A Man's Best Friend, don't you think?"

"So, let me get this right," Indy pulled a face, "you spend most of your time down here, because a pair of social misfits over feed themselves, and you?"

"And Purditta my fine flat mate," Mackison glanced upwards again, "if you look to the left you'll see her curled up on a cushion. Unlike me, she prefers to be spoon fed and petted, even uses the same bathroom sink as them, gets away with peeing but not a

13

number two." The snuffling came again. "Up there we do as we please, but I get bored you see." Mackison pointed to a plastic drain pipe. "There's something about the danger down here!"

"So, you sleep beside the bins…?" Charlie was confused.

"Course not, but if I'm too full up to climb, I just go and sit in the road."

Charlie pulled a puzzled face.

"I'm not insured at the minute, so, Miguel, comes down to collect and carry me up you see."

A loud squealing and the subject suddenly changed.

"Sounds like Vermin," said Gigs, "and talk of the town…"

Vermin scurried towards them. Panting, he stopped beside the bins. "Den caught me in the cheese box. He thought I was a wild rat and tried to exterminate me with some spray." Vermin got his breath, "I didn't hang around!"

"Who the heck is this?" Mackison mused. "And who's Den?"

"This," Charlie confirmed, "is Vermin! Dens, our owner!"

"You have a wild rat as a friend?" Mackison moved his butt backwards, disgust displayed, his face grew wrinkly, his eyes cold and cagey.

"He's sound," said Charlie. "Admittedly a bit rough, but the best buddy a cat could have!" Taking Vermin by the chin, Charlie pointed it upwards. "Say hello, to the balcony bums!"

"Err, what are they?" Vermin pulled away from Charlie.

14

The blubbers of Bendina…?" Mackison didn't like his owners.

"Bendina…?" The, cats all synchronized in surprise.

"Yeah it's the name of this village." Mackison eyed Vermin with curiosity.

Still staring at the state of the two on the balcony, Vermin chuckled. "Shame that fat guy wasn't fitter, he could help us find, and lower a rope to rescue Balloo."

"He…" Mackison swallowed the last of his scraps, wouldn't help you, he hates anything accept alcohol." he rubbed his paws together. "Wait here." Mackison scuffled away and like a large Koala bear, climbed the drain pipe and pulled himself onto the balcony. Five minutes later he returned with a tow rope that he handed to Charlie. "Mandy bought it him for Christmas. He doesn't use it, but will moan if anyone else does, so bring it back before he notices it gone please."

The cats took the rope and began retracing their steps. They had just turned the corner of their street when they saw Den stood in the road. Still looking for the rat that he'd sent on its way he was furious. Frightened, he might spot them, the cats made a beeline for the wall. Tip toeing along it, they stopped not far from the house. Still, slumped and sulking below was Balloo. The cats threw down the rope, scrunching her eyes shut like a big, girls, blouse, Balloo fumbled for it. Heaving, the three cats and Vermin pulled on it, allowing, her to walk up the wall. Once safely upon the ledge, they all sat and looked over their side of the wall. Mackison, not wanting to help, but inquisitive as to the goings on, had followed. He watched the cats and rat with interest before spotting Trike the other side of the wall.

"You brought a three-legged dog with you?" Mackison blurted before moving up to watch Trike trundle some more. "God, you lot are weird."

"He's ok," said, Charlie, "bit of a chuckle at times, but not a bad dog really."

"Seems almost sadistic, there's a place on the hill for crippled and cruelty cases, he might be better off there."

"What place?" Charlie had never heard of any such place in his entire life.

"Supposed to be some sort of sanctuary for the less fortunate animals," Mackison mused, "but I've heard it's more like an asylum."

"And you want us to take Trike there?" Charlie suddenly appeared protective, his voice full of protest, he threw Mackison a nasty glare.

"Why on earth not?" Mackison didn't see a problem with his suggestion.

"I'm going off you faster than fast, fur ball." Charlie snarled feral style.

"Yeah we didn't bring him to Spain to see him suffer!" It was Vermin. "Your attitude stinks!"

"Well, then, why did you bring him here?" Mackison suddenly realized he was out of order and softened. "Look I'm not entirely sure what they do on the hill. Maybe, we should all pay it a personal visit, go see for ourselves."

"So, you'll take us there?" Charlie insisted after the uncalled insult.

"Now wait a minute," Vermin snorted, "we don't even know what's in there."

"Exactly!" Feeling his feral side surface, Charlie raised a paw to silence him, then, the others, before they too piped up. "It will be an adventure."

"Perhaps…" Mackison was apprehensive, "what's in it for me?"

"Friends, you, big moth ball, seems you buy the only ones you have. How about making some real ones, and losing some weight while at it? Well, you gonna lead the way or what?"

"Be by the bins, tomorrow at ten." With that, Mackison took one last look at Trike, turned, and tiptoed away.

"I thought he'd want to be more than just a science diet supplier!" Charlie chuckled.

"Anything must be better than being so bored." Vermin made them laugh until they reached the window.

Apart from Trike and Poo, the living room was empty. Upstairs, Charlie found Becky sleeping. A moment later he heard the engine of Dens car. Making the most of the peace, the cats curled up on the cane furniture and slept.

A Clash of Culture

Opening his eyes, the first thing Charlie saw was Trike. He didn't look healthy, had a dull aura, was under the weather and weak. This in mind, Charlie kept his usual banter to himself and fetched him milk from the kitchen. Placing it before his nose, the scent waft into his nostrils slowly bringing him around. While Trike indulged, Charlie, had other ideas.

"Right you lot," he stirred the cats, "let's get going." Leering into a large plant pot, he woke Vermin, "c'mon, you too."

Back from his trip, Denis was in the hallway preparing to paint an old cupboard. Preoccupied with choosing the correct brushes and colours, the cats were able to sneak past him without being seen. Once out the front, they scampered into the street. True to his word, Mackison was waiting beside the bins. A map in hand, he wore a pair of tartan sun glasses and matching hat.

Charlie eyed him with amusement. "A swim suit and you'd look like a beach babe."

"Are you saying, I look like a girl, tin ribs?" Mackison snapped the map together.

"No," Charlie glanced up onto the balcony where Mandy was sat, "but, you're exactly how I imagine her to look in a tartan bikini."

"Are you saying I'm a bum?" Mackison hissed! Intimidated by

18

the insinuation, he failed to see the funny side of it, even less hearing them laugh at his expense. Snapping a bone in two, he sat up straight.

"Country cats come to play the clown in our feral town!" On his toes he pranced towards the ravine. "Well, let's see how you fair…!"

Putting a lid on their laughter, the cats crept after him and down the first of the vertical banks. Levelling out, each one offered better traction to their feet, than the last. Canyon conquered, the cats and vermin, looked up from the gorge. Tacky tin roofs, surrounded by chain link fence, a wall of wire reached into the sky.

"There you go," Mackison sat down to rest his feet, "one dismal sanctuary."

"It looks like Alcatraz!" Charlie gazed in astonishment.

"You what…" Indy pulled a bewildered face.

"I saw a film with Den once," Charlie muttered, "it was about a human prison."

"Well," Vermin, retorted, "there certainly not enough of them!"

Mackison coughed drily, "I've never been this close before and don't know, what's up there. But, if you want to carry on…?"

"We've come this far," Charlie hesitated, "we, may as well be brave, and have a go at getting up there."

Taking hold of shrubs and boulders, the cats climbed and clung to the fence. Teetering on its ledge, the terrified cats were face to face with a dozen tigers. Docile, the big cats didn't move.

"They're either drugged or brain damaged!" Vermin couldn't believe his eyes. Totally shut down, their souls had been wrung.

"This is no sanctuary!" Charlie fumed, Then, gazing beyond the tigers, he spied slim alleyways. Accompanied by various animal noises, it sounded like a mad house. "How sad for the wildlife, I've watched enough documentaries with Den to know when something is internally dead!"

Gigs shuddered, felt her hair stand up on end, and tears enter her eyes, "Endangered, species, aren't they?"

"Exactly…!" Charlie, exclaimed.

"Shall we…" Moving to his right, Mackison had found a loose bit of fence and lifted it. Holding it open, he indicated for the cats to entered.

Further in they saw lifeless lions and poorly kept porcupines, but it was the black leopard who spoke first. "They are prisoners in the confines of their own bodies now."

"What do you mean?" Charlie delved.

"They've all been used and abused," a sigh left the leopard, "some, even subjected to experiments. Enter, but be careful of the humans as you go."

They trundled along the path, stopping every few minutes to offer their sympathy to the suffering animals behind the bars. Some five minutes on and they found themselves mingling with, paying visitors. Accepted as nothing other than strays, the cats were completely ignored and had a free reign to roam. As they turned a corner, Vermin stopped dead in his tracks. It was a glass tank, crammed inside it, injured and sore, at least forty odd rats fought for space.

"I know we stink," Vermin defended, "but the fumes leaving that tank are atrocious, a man-made disease just waiting to escape."

"It's called weil's disease!" Mackison moved on before Vermin could rip into him, "and, there isn't anything well, about them!"

Vermin picked up a rock and smashed the glass, leaping over the broken bits, the rats fled.

"Are you mad?" Charlie winced." I can't believe you Vermin!" Hoping they hadn't been heard, Charlie led the others away. Halting on a bend, they all gazed ahead. Catching up, Vermin watched the human visitors with hatred. A python seemed to attract much of their attention and a pool of polluted turtles gained a few, "aahhhhs."

"They should be in the lake," Balloo said to Gigs.

"We'll get some buckets and come back another day!" Gigs agreed.

"Come on," Charlie didn't want to be caught, "standing and staring will only generate unwanted attention."

A few yards further on, and a sign caught Charlie's, attention. Perched beyond a set of railings, a cage sat snug on the hill. Demented from boredom, stood four chimps. Heads rocking from side to side their eyes darted up and down.

"Can you read it?" Charlie looked at Mackison, then again at the sign...

"It says they've been rescued from an experimental lab." Mackison swallowed hard. "They have been here ten years today." One of the chimps threw an arm out of the bars. A plea for help crystal clear.

"What on earth can we do for them?" Balloo, blew her nose and wiped an oncoming tear away. To her left was a white lion, with stripes, "A hybrid," she bellowed. With that, she burst into tears.

"Some sanctuary…!" Vermin was vicious towards Mackison.

"Hang on," said Charlie, "we can't blame him, he's never been here before."

"No, but, he wanted us to bring Trike here!"

Without answering, Charlie was drawn to voices down the aisle. Through human legs, he weaved towards the entrance where a man was holding his hand out to the oncoming public. Taking a breath, the cats observed him in more detail.

"Thank you," the man repeated to the public, "the more we make the more creature comforts we can offer our furry friends."

"Is this guy for real?" Charlie couldn't believe his ears. Several notes passed through the man's hands, the gestures to keep the change, obvious and ongoing. "This place is made of misery and they're paying to enter and enjoy it!" Charlie was mad. He rushed forward but was caught by Indy.

"Careful bro, you don't want to become a permanent fixture here, do you?" Indy pointed to a cage on their right. Inside, similar in size, sat several hybrid cats. "No point in making a nuisance of yourself yet. Let's get this one right."

"I had no idea…" Mackison suddenly felt overwhelmed with anxiety. Quickly, he buried his head in his paws.

"It's not your fault," insisted, Gigs, "it merely confirms what a deplorable creature man is."

"Shall we go?" Mackison, had, had enough.

Charlie didn't answer. Instead, he cast his mind back to his kitten hood. Quickly, recalling, when he and Indy, had been locked in a cage with their sister, Samba. Suddenly, visions of her flying around, looking down on him and Indy, materialized. Charlie knew what it was to be locked up, but not the atrocities around him.

"I've, never seen such cruelty." Charlie eventually blurted.

"Not nice, I give you that!" Mackison mulled over his own statement.

"This," Charlie sneered, "is a clash of animal culture cleverly concocted to make money for man!"

"I have no cents." A woman said rummaging through her hand bag for coins to donate on her way out.

"You have no sense at all!" Charlie screeched aloud.

"I usually have enough change to leave a tip," she exclaimed to the man collecting, "but not today. I am sorry."

"I'll give you a tip," Charlie belched, "sod off, and don't come back you, old ignominy."

"Let's leave," said Gigs, "I sense trouble brewing and were not ready for a riot."

Turning the cats saw an iguana. Sun burnt its skin was sore and speckled. A little further on they stood before what seemed to be an empty enclosure. Then out of the shadows came four bears. Feet pushed through the bars, they gazed at the cats. Unafraid of the giant paws, Charlie touched the rough pad there.

"Can you fetch us some water?" The bear spoke wearily.

"Where from…?" Charlie asked.

The bear pointed to a tap on the left. Beside it sat a dirty bucket. The cats filled and dragged it to the cage. The bears drank until their face fur was saturated and their stomachs full. Several buckets later they began to slow down. Lips watered, one of them spoke in a better tone.

"Unlike many here, we still actually have our marbles."

"Marbles…" Charlie was confused.

"He means he's not brain dead yet." Vermin nudged Charlie.

Saddened, Charlie changed the subject. "When was the last time you ate?"

"Yesterday, but stale bread, pizza and peppers, eventually makes you sick."

"We'll be back," Charlie was now on a mission, "and when we do, we'll bring you something better than fish."

Down, and despondent, the cats left the so-called sanctuary, with heavy hearts…

Village Vagabonds

"Well, there was nothing idyllic about that place!" Charlie screeched at the darkening sky, then to the others as they made their way back over the wafers of earth.

"So…" Mackison asked Charlie with more interest than he was letting on. "Do you have any ideas on how to solve the situation?"

"A good night's sleep," Charlie frowned, "then, I'll give it to you!"

Charlie churned his findings over all night. Havoc reaping horror, he finally fell asleep at 5am. Still fresh when he woke up, his thoughts continued from where they'd signed off. The animals he'd seen were in desperate need of nurturing and nourishment, but, more than anything else, their freedom! How, Charlie had no idea, but his subconscious gnawed at him like a dog with a bone. Charlie was free and therefore had more power than those behind bars. Distraught by it all, he decided to hold a meeting with Mackison and if in agreement, the feral's too.

"Come on you lot," seeing Vermin tucked up inside a plant pot, Charlie, chimed a pen upon it, "wake up!"

"If you don't stop tapping my China," Vermin shrieked, "I'll sock you in the chin!"

Gigs gave Charlie a scornful glance, she loved her slumber. Indy pulled back his eye patch, squinted in irritation and pushed it back over his eye.

Balloo let out a loud burp. "I was dreaming of fresh prawns."

26

"Well they will have to wait!" Charlie pressed.

"They won't do that, they can be funny you know!"

"Well they've never made me laugh!" Charlie mocked. "C'mon, you've gotta pull your weight!"

"If you don't mind," said Balloo, "I'm trying to lose some."

"Being funny doesn't suit you," Charlie sniggered, "so get up."

Climbing out of his plant pot, cheese between his claws, Vermin listened to the lot of them. Taking one last nibble, he then tossed the surplus aside. "Don't go a bundle on this Spanish blue stuff it's more like soft sick. So, what's the plan then Charlie. Are we putting together a rescue operation or what?"

"The thought had crossed my mind," Charlie grinned, "but to make it happen, we need that posh Mackison and his mates."

"What on earth for?" Balloo expressed a look of sheer horror.

"Because," Charlie stammered, "not only does the great ball of blue fluff know the area, but, he has authority amongst the ferals."

Charlie heard Becky, getting out of bed. The litter tray was empty. "Damn," he sighed, "She'll know we've been out, unless someone goes?" The, seriousness of Charlie, entertained Vermin no end. "Look I know it's not what you wanna hear, but our freedom depends on one of you filling a tray. Charlie raised his eyelashes. "Come on, someone must need a number two?"

"Certainly not in front of you..." Balloo squirmed.

"Right you lot, let's go and leave her to it." Charlie leapt onto the windowsill and glanced back. "Make a mess and shake it all about, won't you?" With that him and the others, disappeared.

"The days only just begun and it's already dysfunctional." Gigs sounded disgruntled.

"It's the only way to solve the problem!" Vermin followed the cats out and onto the wall where they waited...

Balloo appeared, shook her butt in a playful manner and leapt accurately, onto the wall beside the others. Once over it, they wandered briskly up the hill. They had just reached the school, when a stray dog appeared and chased them into the undergrowth. Five minutes later they managed to join Mackison.

"How about a jail break for those poor prisoners on the hill...?" Charlie couldn't believe that he was suggesting it, but he was, and his intentions were indeed honorable.

Mackison put down his bone, both paws preening his whiskers of fish, he smirked. Though a pompous cat, his compassionate side was beginning to smolder and show.

"They..." he glanced up at Miguel and Mandy are going out. "When they do, come up. I'll then give the feral's a nod to openly discuss our options."

Mackison moved towards the drain pipe, taking a hold of it, he hoisted himself upwards and clambered onto his balcony. Brushing through Mandy's legs he pawed a cushion until it was plumped up.

Thirty minutes passed before, Miguel and Mandy appeared in the car park. The cats watched them waddle towards a Land Rover and drive away. The weather was hot, and Gigs struggled to climb the drainpipe.

"Oh, come on," said Charlie shoving her upwards, "if Mac, can climb it you can!"

There's a knack to it that you'll need to master." Mackison shouted down at them.

"Piece of cake," Charlie said, instantly wishing he hadn't."

Tumbling down, Gig's hit the ground with a thud. "Go on then clever clogs," she bellowed at Charlie, "show us all how to do it!"

At first, the plastic pipe seemed almost impossible to grip. Not wanting to lose face, Charlie spat on all four pads, clapped them tightly to the pipe and pulled. Back feet fighting his body weight, Charlie was weary on reaching the balcony, but didn't let on to anyone. The air conditioning inside was inviting, cooling the cats as they one by one arrived. Astonished at such luxuries, they tiptoed across a golden tiled floor, checked out the science diet and couldn't resist taking a peep in the bathroom sink.

"There's nothing to see in there," Mackison cooed, "not at this time of day, anyway." Wishing he hadn't made the bad habits of his flat mate public, Mac pointed at her. Perfectly groomed, face down on a pillow, only a pink bow on her head could be seen. "This is Purditta," he finally frowned.

"Princess Purditta, if you don't mind." She scorned at him. Speaking with perfection, the faint smell of perfume wafted from her fur. A beautiful glam cat her owners had not hung back in the financial department. Love at first sight, Charlie had to control his emotions. Far too good for him, she would never fancy a cheeky feral such as him. A mischievous twinkle in them, her electric blue eyes, examined the visitors. Vermin, spotted, she pulled a vulgar face.

"Right," Mackison said snatching back the attention, let's get down to business. Fortunately for us, some of the hardest moggies in town have offered us their assistance." He moved towards the balcony and whistled. A few moments later four mangy ferals arrived. Built like tanks they lumbered over the railings, bringing the smell of the street and fleas with them.

Purditta pranced across the room. "Hello, boys, how are you all?"

"Been better," the largest scratched a bald patch on his head, "a lot better!"

Purditta gave him a tin of flea spray before approaching the balcony railings. In the car park below was a fine faced, shapely Staffordshire.

"What a powerful dog," said, Purditta.

"That's cos she is a right old dog," said another of the feral's, "she's had several litters over the years!"

"Now now…Its not her fault if the owners don't neuter." Purditta perched herself on one of the wider plant pots. Wriggling her bottom into the blue flowers, she got comfortable. Checking her nails were clean, she then placed her chin on her paws. "So," she gave, Charlie an encouraging glance, "Mac, says, you want to do a jail break, help the animals escape and expose the owner?"

"That's right," Charlie bravely pushed his way forward till sat in front of her. "Is there anything you can tell me that might help?" He directed his conversation to the gangly gangster cats all around him.

"We know the place is dirty," lifting the flea spray the feral raised an arm, "too disgusting, even for us." He, smirked.

"A bit of togetherness, teamwork is what's needed," another of them interjected.

"It would help!" Vermin ventured nearer the ferals.

"You're ok," Croft, the largest of the lot croacked, "we've already eaten!" Vermin shrunk, "joke, it's a joke! Mac said you lot were different. That you didn't see the harm in having a rat friend."

"Each to their own," another gestured using the last of the flea spray on his hackles.

"Come on…" Charlie moved closer to Vermin, "I think he's pretty brave facing you lot."

"Here, here," the feral's agreed.

"So," Charlie changed the subject, "if, we manage to free them, what will we do with them?"

"Look around you," Mackison mused at the mountains, "wouldn't it be something to set them free out there?"

"Yes, it would," Gigs agreed, "if we could trick the humans for a day or two, it would allow the animals to elope to other areas."

"Purrrrr-fect." Charlie clapped his paws together, "we just need to develop a diversion."

31

"Anything in mind then…?" Croft, the craziest, of the feral's asked him.

"No, but something will come. For now, let's just concentrate on getting them out."

Eat your heart out," Vermin grimaced, "were about to make a historical mark."

The Cats Whiskers

Removing herself from the railings, Purditta set about cutting cheese and pouring Irish cream. A plate of fish flavoured crackers, she was the perfect host. Ideas exchanged, a proper plan began to emerge. Too much to take in at once, Purditta took out a pen and pad.

"You can write?" Impressed, Charlie lit up like a lamp.

"I had a Persian pen pal." Purditta didn't look up from the pad, instead, she spoke aloud.

"Pen knife, lock picks, easing oil, balaclavas, bolt crops, camera and antidote." The word, antidote, caused a stir. Purditta looked up and smiled, "just in case of any accidental bites." She continued to flick her pen back and forth, filling the pad accordingly.

"I say we go there tonight! From what you saw, freedom can't arrive soon enough." The feral put down his glass and lowered his voice, "I'd like to pee on the person responsible."

"A dude like that, deserves nothing less than a number two!" The sink springing to mind, Charlie quickly looked at Purditta who blushed before standing her ground.

"Well, I could make an exception." Her comment amused all present.

"They won't be able to fend for themselves straight away," said another feral, "even we, still have to hide from the hunters."

33

"Then, we shall have to show our big brothers how to hunt all over again won't we...?" Purditta leapt elegantly to her feet and brushed past Charlie. Provocatively, she stood between the two patio doors.

A vision of her in a pair of hot pants leading the lions across the land was pushing his buttons. Charlie was older and more mature, had never considered canoodling with another cat. Not until now. Emotions rising from deep inside, she had, stirred his senses, and made him see stars. And even though he didn't feel good enough for her, he couldn't help but dream. Charlie felt himself blush. Deliberately pointing beyond the car park, he created a diversion before becoming a red beacon. "We'll meet on that hill, say around seven?"

"Seven it is," said the feral gangsters.

"What about the equipment we need?" enquired a feral. "We'll need tools to work with."

Mackison lifted the box he'd been sat on. Inside it, was all the items listed by Purditta. Spotting a hand saw, Balloo grabbed at it. Easing oil, wire nips and pen knifes a compass and some pliers were all quickly removed from the box.

"Very Impressive," Charlie, intoned. He then glared straight at Vermin, "will you spray the padlocks with easing oil?"

"You got it boss!" Vermin caught the can, the glint in his eye all good as he imagined the cages opening.

"Balloo," Charlie clapped eyes on her, "will you and Gigs inform the animal inmates what's happening?"

"Our pleasure...!" Both cats purred.

"Indy, can you keep watch while the feral cats cut the locks."

"With what…?" Indy asked.

"These…" The blades nearly as frightening as him, Croft, prized a pair of bolt croppers open and shut.

Mackison began laughing.

"What is it?" Charlie enquired.

"The thought of Miguel's face when he thinks he's been burgled of his belongings!"

"Give me five…" Charlie raised a paw to Mackison, "if you're in agreement fur ball, you and I can take care of the human responsible for the suffering."

"You got it!" Mackison gloated.

"What have you got in mind?" Purditta gave Charlie a gorgeous grin.

"Once we know what we're up against, I guess, a little improvisation will be needed."

"Am I to be excluded from such a historical excursion?" Aware of Charlie's attraction towards her, Perditta tapped her claws on the wall beside him. Quite taken by her comment, Charlie was slow to react.

"Well, if you insist," Charlie coughed, trying to stay tight button lipped, "I'm, sure Mackison, will find something for you to do."

"If you could stop painting your nails for five minutes," chomping on a large lump of cheese, Mackison mused, "you might actually be of some use to us!"

"And perhaps if you stopped eating you might shrink," Purditta pouted her lips, "now, how about a toast!"

"To what...?" Mackison swallowed his brie.

"Friendship and freedom...!" A chink of glasses and Purditta politely slurped her cream.

"Here, here," A cats, choir echoed throughout the flat.

The idea of her, and her new hair-do, fumbling across the terrain, certainly seemed to please the cats.

"Right!" Chuffed, Charlie, put his glass on the table, "we best get these tools hidden on the hillside before the alcoholics arrive home." He then gazed at his lot, "we'd best then make sure were home for tea."

"Good idea..." The cats grabbed all they could carry and left through the front door. Crossing the car park, they unloaded it all onto the hillside and hurried home.

Becky was in the kitchen, "I need a new sink installed," the cats heard her complain. Sneaking past the open window they climbed through theirs and waited for supper. "It's always the same when I need something new," Becky grumbled, "but not when you want something!"

Just then the telephone bleeped. Pleased of the diversion, Denis sighed in relief as she hurried off to answer it. The tone in her voice changed and the sink no longer seemed important. Denis knew it wasn't a social call.

"What is it?" His tone softened, even sounded, sympathetic.

"The vet from England just confirmed the tests I did for Trike."

"And…?"

"He has cancer," she sobbed.

On hearing the news, the cats entered the room.

"Maybe it's a blessing." Denis blundered, "I mean we have been struggling to cover his costs."

"How could you?" The cats followed Becky into the front room where Trike was sleeping.

His wheel removed, they suddenly saw how much weight he'd lost. How small he was compared to how his big breed should be. He was a crumpled, crippled heap of unhappiness. Sat beside him, the prospect of losing another friend all too much, Poo was silent. The cats were speechless, so much misery in such a short time.

"Well, that explains why you have been looking so sorry for yourself." Charlie sighed. "Is there anything I can do, you know, before you go…?"

Trike raised his head, "I hear you're organizing a jail break. Is it true?"

"News travels fast, yes, it is." Charlie perked up.

"Then stop feeling sorry for me and put my wheel back in place. I'd like to see the animals set free."

But…" it was Poo.

"No if's, no buts," said Trike, "I'm a dead dog walking anyway, what harm can it do, other than bring me some happiness."

"Have him out of here before six," Charlie said to Poo. "Can you get to the rock tiers beside the bins?" Poo nodded, "Wait there till we arrive."

Tormented by his inner turmoil, Trike raised his head and managed a smile. Resigned to the thought of reincarnation, he was ready for it. Tears breaking through, Becky carried her broken heart into the kitchen. Consoled by Denis, who expressed the upmost compassion towards his wife, and dying companion, she eventually stopped crying.

"Makes a change for that little creep to show some concern…" Charlie spat.

"Even he has his moments," Poo replied.

"Hmm, memories and moments, is about all he does have." Charlie scowled. Winking at Poo, he made off towards the cat pantry where he gathered some nail clippers, a pair of tweezers and a toothbrush from the shelf. Taking down his bum bag, he filled and fastened it to his waste. Turning around, Charlie found himself face to face, with Vermin. "You never know what might come in handy," Charlie pulled on Vermin's dungaree clips and smirked.

"Aren't you going to brush your hair?" Vermin asked him.

"What for…?" Charlie snapped, while at the same time wishing he would mind his own business.

"She'll prefer vanity, to some of the vulgar you sometimes express." Vermin sniggered.

Charlie was both irritated and intrigued by the comment.

"So, what do you suggest stud?" An air of arrogance about him, Charlie glared at Vermin for answers.

"She aint a mangy moggie. Best mind your manners, comb your hair and curb your language."

"I was just getting around to that!" Charlie smirked. He then swanned into the spare room, stuffed his face with cat biscuits and deliberately did a dump in the litter tray. Afterwards he joined the others for a cat nap. It was an eerie echo, that woke him.

"A little more leverage," he heard Poo mutter, "And we're there." With each pull she made, a whimper was heard from Trike. Intrigued and nosey, Charlie crept next door. There, alone on her own, Poo struggled to fully fasten the wheel straps together.

"Here, let me help." Taking the nylon in his teeth, Charlie gave it the tug needed to reach the buckle. The wheel in place, and Trike began to push it around the front room. Fear and pain clearly expressed, his eyes were hollow, the folds of skin surrounding his eyes aged and arid. The once muscular Trike, now meek and minute, it hurt to see him fading away. Only hours gone by, eyes secretly misted in disappointment, Trike was distant and dismal. Nonetheless, he stood proud, taking everything in. Poo opened the front door for him. Holding it ajar, she watched him wheel himself out onto the street. A few seconds later the latch slammed shut. Through the window Charlie watched the two departing dogs slumber up the hill. The wheel of diminishing time turning with

Trike's every step, life for Charlie, suddenly took on a whole new meaning.

"Come on you lot," he called to the others, "there's loads to do, and even more reason, to do it now. When your days are numbered like Trike's, you don't have time to sleep!"

Up in an instant, the cats ate the dinner Becky had put out, grabbed what they needed and left through the window. Making their way to the meeting point, they were pleased to see Poo and Trike already there. Absorbing the picturesque hills before them, Trike appeared peaceful. Stone gullies like sleeping crocodiles, random foliage and cream boulders, the journey wasn't going to be easy for Trike. Easing the apprehension on Poo's face, they pointed out some longer, but flatter routes for them to use. Ten minutes later, Mackison and the ferals arrived. Tooled up, they were ready to take on the world.

"And who have we here then?" One of the ferals examined, Trike, then Poo.

Charlie explained the situation, and how Trike's last wish was too witness, the event. Taking a step back, Mackison could not believe the rapid demise of their dear friend in such a short space of time.

"I don't know what to say," one of the feral frowned.

"How about let's get going!" Trike's eyes lit up for the first time in a long time. "If you make this happen at least I'll have some memories to take with me!"

Fears of him slowing them up immediately forgotten, the cats were glad to have him on board.

"Go on," Poo smiled, "go ahead! If, Trike tires, I will stop and wait with him."

"Right," Mackison reached for the first of the mud meringues, "let's do it."

"Lead the way, fur ball." Charlie threw Mackison a playful glance.

Long legs swinging from left to right, Mackison marched like a proud baboon. Behind him, a clan of country cats, one rat and four ferals followed. They had just reached the third layer, when...

"Wait for me."

Charlie and the others turned to see Purditta. Dressed in a pin striped cat suit and matching head band, she pranced down the hill. Charlie was eager to embrace her, but afraid of rejection, stood rooted to the ground instead.

"Glad you could make it," was all that came out of Charlie. "Right," he waved to Mackison, "it's time to turn misery into a match one mission."

 # The Raid

Purditta and Poo hit it off straight away. Either side of Trike, they encouraged him over the easiest terrain possible. Momentum gathered, Trike found a new lease of life, enjoyed the passing birds and engaged with a hare who shared a few seconds of time with him. Mackison and the others growing closer, Trike caught them up. The level beneath the sanctuary in sight, it was partially bald.

"What on earth has happened here?" Gig's couldn't believe how much it had changed in only a few days. Parched, the grass had a horrible yellow appearance.

"Weed killer," Mackison frowned, "it keeps the undergrowth free from creepy crawlies."

"Why would they want to kill grass in a country it never normally grows?" Gig's was shocked.

"Because," Croft, vented, "humans are completely twisted in here," he pointed to his head, "Potty, botty, totally grotty."

Just then the fence above rattled. Faces pressed like pastry in cake cutters, the tigers gazed downwards. "They look worse for wear." His own bad experience surfacing, Indy shuddered.

Picking up on his vibes, Charlie felt protective. "We can't change the past, but today we're going to change their future."

Purditta and Poo both gave him the thumbs up. Settled in the sun, Trike felt content.

"You'll keep watch, won't you?"

Perditta put her arm around Trike and nodded.

Aspiring to leave some-sort of visible path behind them, the cats removed rocks, clawed at the undergrowth and trod it into an aisle. Twenty minutes later, they were face to face with the tigers.

"How do you fancy a little freedom?" The first to go under the fence, Vermin passed them and sprayed the lock with easing oil.

"Where will we go?" The tigers voice was hoarse and dry.

"Down there..." Croft began cutting their chain link with the bolt cutters. The ferals pulled, folding it backwards until big enough for them to fit through. "Follow our tracks, you'll find Purditta at the bottom." Traumatized, the tigers didn't move a muscle. "Hurry it along," Croft wanted them out as fast as possible.

"Leave them to think about it!" Charlie led the cats through the opening, past the tigers and towards their lock. Unlike the fence, it was rust riddled. Through gritted teeth, the cats eventually broke it. An exit in place, they tackled the second cage. Porcupines free, Charlie pointed them towards the tiger exit. Going ahead of Charlie, Gigs and Balloo, explained to the waiting animals, what was going to happen. While some thought they were dreaming and hesitated, others, found their feet and fled. Ferals fast at cutting, Charlie and Mackison, headed for the main entrance. Gates locked, area empty, it was eerie. Taking out a toothpick, Charlie bit on it. Moving to his left, he saw the outline of a square cage, not far from it, the door to the house.

"I knew it was here somewhere!" Charlie said to Mackison.

"Let me out and I'll help you." A lion cub in the cage yawned.

"You've been in there, haven't you?" Charlie moved closer to the cub.

"It isn't nice!" Cold, the cub shivered.

Charlie whistled for Vermin, to bring his oil over. An armed feral, not far behind, a chink was herd and the lock hit the ground.

"He should be drunk by now!" The cub scampered out and towards the door, pushed it open and entered.

"Tell me more." Torch lighting the way, Charlie was in close pursuit.

"He spends most of the takings on himself, though you'd never believe it by the state of this place." The cub scurried down the hallway, "this way," he turned right, "I will take you to the culprit."

Charlie tried to ignore the strong scent of urine that stung his eyes and settled on his tongue. "Why, do I get the feeling I'm not going to like this?"

The cub didn't answer. Instead, he took a u bend and pointed to a pantry type area. All dark, Charlie shone the torch inside it. Faces still and stern, three monkeys stared out of a cage.

"Don't worry little fellas, you'll soon be free." Charlie flicked the latch up and opened it. Apprehensive and afraid, the monkeys made no attempt to leave the cage.

"Let the shock of freedom sink in." The cub moved on, "they have been here, a long time."

"What if, like, the tigers, they don't budge." Charlie fretted.

"The choice is theirs," Mackison had caught them up.

44

A few yards on and a caged parrot pecked at an empty water tray. Charlie flipped the door open, but the bird began to create. "Let me be, let me be, this is my world can't you see!"

"A game bird giving it," Charlie was shocked, "get out, and get real." Charlie shooed the bird out of the cage. "There's a whole world out there, go on, get going!"

The cub swung left. A moment later the sound of human snoring was heard. Heavy farting combined with old sweat, their eyes outlined a well-used, flea bitten mattress. Sprawled across it was the skinny corpse of their bad guy. Skin aged and arid, at least two weeks of stubble growth smothered his chin, filling his cheeks too. Like litter, a scattering of tatty clothes, hole ridden shoes, broken braces and bottles, surrounded the bed. The stench of sweat, alongside the foul breath, moving in and out of his mouth, made the overall smell quite putrid.

"That's one ugly boat race." Charlie whimpered in dismay.

"A filthy pig, if ever I saw one!" Mackison sighed. The rug beneath his feet looked like it had been dragged through the street after a torrential bout of rain, and the wall paper hung in ugly twists that twirled into dreadlocks. On the bedside cabinet was a broken lamp. A walk-in wardrobe housed more than just tatty clothes. Dozens of bin bags, tied and stored, bulged at the seams. Untying the top of one, Charlie shone his torch inside. Astounded at the contents he, and the lion cub, gasped.

Cash, hundreds, thousands even, all salted away for a rainy day had been hidden.

"Right first things first." Charlie, handed the others a sack each, tiptoeing out of the room they all hurried towards the entrance. Outside, they gulped oxygen in the hope of cleaning their lungs.

"Shall I get Purditta to help?" Mackison was always quick off the mark, especially when it came to valuables.

"Since everybody else is busy, I suppose you best had!" Charlie watched him disappear. Already on his way back for another sack, Charlie scampered after the lion cub. They were on their third run, when there she was, with Mackison.

"Well, its just incredible!" Purditta, counted seven sacks. Are there any more?"

Charlie waved five claws up and introduced the lion cub.

"Poverty is one thing," Purditta referred to the state of the place, "but this is a deliberate, act of personal gain."

Charlie pushed two sacks towards her. "Can you manage them!"

"Of course." Purditta shone, "Gosh, these animals have been through it!"

"Don't worry about that," Charlie said adoringly, "Now, can I leave this cash in your capable hands or have I got to do everything your highness?" Charlie enjoyed teasing her.

"Of, course you may country cat!" Purditta played along, scooped up two of the sacks and pranced away.

A fleeting deer crossing her path, Purditta found herself, face to face with one of the ferals. "some heavy stuff's been going on here man." She puffed.

"What do you mean?" The feral loved it when she spoke slang.

"I'm not sure yet," she shook a bag, "but someone's been saving for a rainy day, and rain on him it will!"

"Dya mean were rich?"

"Maybe…?"

"Does that mean I can ask you out?" A new suit in mind and the feral chanced his luck.

"I'll take you out!" Interrupting them, a hybrid hit on the feral.

"Looks like you're already spoken for." Purditta chucked the sack over her shoulder and laughed in amusement.

Still in their cage, the three monkeys refused to budge. "You lot might eat nuts, but you don't have to act like them!" Mackison tried to make them see sense.

In the less, than basic kitchen, Charlie rummaged through a junk draw, removing certain items, he handed some of them to lion. Loaded, they then made their way back to the owner. The last three sacks safely in the hallway, Charlie removed a long tube of glue and glared at lion.

"If, you don't mind getting your paws dirty I'm going to ask you to roll him over."

"You got it!" Pushing, the pile of human bones, to one side, the cub watched the super glue go to work. Gently easing the man down the cub saw the sheets stick to him.

"Now for that ugly boat race," whispered Charlie.

47

Dabbing his dirty face with the glue nozzle, Charlie then sliced open the pillow and pulled out a bunch of feathers. Shoe laces tied together, trousers torn and glued either side of the mattress, the man was beginning to look like a half-prepped Christmas turkey. Only he wasn't free range, he was from a bad batch. Taking a rope from the wall, Charlie wrapped it around the man. Waste, ankles and chest secured, he began to slow down. Mobile switched off, Charlie threw it down the toilet.

"There, that should keep him quiet for some time." Charlie bowed awkwardly to the lion cub, a gesture of respect regarding his suffering. "Right then, we best get the last sacks and get going."

Charlie was pleased to see the monkey cage empty as they passed. Outside, Mackison was out of breath.

"They wouldn't budge," he heaved, "I had to carry them one by one down to Purditta and Poo. Heavy too, they were!"

"Well done…" Charlie patted him on the back.

"No sweat! Apart from the chimps, most of the animals are on the move!"

"Can you manage these?" Charlie handed him the last of the sacks. "Me, and lion will double check all the animals are gone!"

"You got it!" Mackison made off.

Charlie and lion worked their way back towards the exit. Broken locks on the floor, the empty cages were up lifting. But, hey hang on. Still occupied, cage five expelled heavy breathing and nerves. Inside, shy, and shaky stood two little, lynx. A few kind words and they cruised out of the cage. Moving on, Charlie and the cub clambered up a hill towards four chimps. Full of beans their heads bat back and forth but when Charlie opened the cage they shied away and wouldn't budge. Two minutes later and Vermin arrived.

"Come on, your free." He yelled, we need this place emptied.

"To do what," one of them asked, "we know nothing of the outside world. Where will we go, what, will we eat?"

"A damned sight more than you've been getting in here," Vermin growled, "so climb down and get going, while you can, you big baboons."

"But he comes to feed us at five," the chimp insisted.

"Not tonight he won't!" Charlie balked. "C'mon, it's time you learnt, to feed and fend for yourselves."

"Don't you get it," Vermin scowled, "you're free, free as the birds."

Charlie grew anxious, his paw still on the handle his claws tapped it. "Come on out, there's all sorts of creature comforts to be experienced. We'll hide and help you if need be, till you can cope."

The word *help'* hit a chord and the chimps began to budge. Charlie gave Vermin a high five and made after them. Cagey, the tigers watched a giraffe and some pot-bellied pigs hurry down towards Purditta.

"What are you waiting for?" Charlie shook the wire fence. Running scared, the tigers one by one, finally fled. Charlie was about to give Vermin a pat on the back when a horrible sound grated upon them. Charlie shrugged at Vermin.

"The bears," Vermin squealed, "we forgot the bears."

"Then back we go." Charlie did an about turn.

Vermin snatched the pair of bolt croppers from Croft and followed. Stood before the great grizzlies, Vermin was visibly, hesitant.

"We mean you no harm." Teeth gone, only an abscess in his mouth, the bear was a sorry sight. "Being here has been a battle of wits, without you guys we would have died for sure."

"Not today my friend. Today you learn to play a different game of survival." Arms aiming the spray as if it were a real gun, Vermin shot the padlock. A twist of his hand, a clank of metal and the cage came open. Sores on their feet the bears struggled to stand. Wobbly, they used their limbs properly for the first time in years. The last to leave the enclosure, the youngest bear paused before Charlie and Vermin.

"It's been years, thank you."

"Don't mention it!" His sentence too much to comprehend, Vermin shuddered.

The bear moved uncomfortably, his mangy fur alive with mites they had burrowed big sores in his back. Pulling a face, Charlie couldn't begin to imagine their pain.

"I wondered what had happened to you two!" Hurrying around the bears, Mackison made straight for Charlie. "If you're done, I think we should get away from here!"

The three of them followed the bears to the tiger fence. There, resting their backs against it they watched them lumber down the path to Purditta, Trike and Poo.

"Trike must be feeling pretty good by now!" Charlie crossed his arms and smiled at all the animals around him.

"If you ask me," Mackison moaned, "we've saddled ourselves with a load of geriatrics. I mean just look at them, they will never hunt, you're letting loose a liability."

"Shut up you great sack of spoilt sick!" Vermin squared up to Mackison. "We've enough cash to teach them the foxtrot! Animal therapy, if need be…!"

"Allow me mate." Charlie nudged, Vermin aside until face to face with Mackison. "Now listen to me, you shapeless, shallow minded moron! They need our help, and with or without yours, they're, going to get it!"

"Yeah fluff ball." Vermin snapped vehemently. "How about, you go back to being vigilant instead of vile, and continue being courageous?"

"Here, here…" Charlie was impressed with the vocabulary. "now, Mackison, can you take back your insolence and start using your initiative again."

"I was just scared!" Mackison admitted.

"Of what?" Charlie's ears stood upright.

"Of it all going wrong!"

"Even if it does," Charlie squealed at Mackison, "it's a damned sight better than the hell they've just left behind!"

"Better to die by the hand of nature than the nut back there!" Vermin shuddered.

The three of them leapt down from the drop off and onto the lower level. The last of her posh stories told, Purditta was pleased of their arrival and looked to them for answers. While Charlie put his thinking cap on, Mackison did the same with his sunglasses.

"For now," Charlie glanced at the animals, "I guess it's time to make the split!"

Panic stricken, some of the smallest creatures scarpered towards the undergrowth and away. The big cats, chimps and bears however, looked a little lost.

"Where will we sleep?" Nervous, it was the little bear.

"I'm sure you can make good of all that!" Throwing his arm upwards Croft, referred to the tufts of forestry on the opposite mountain. "Once we get all of you out of sight, and have had a \ rest," he glanced at the other cats, "we will vacate the village, return, and show you how to hunt."

"Just hang about," it was Mackison, "once that idiot in there informs the authorities the hunters will be out. All guns blazing, they will persecute everything especially, pigs."

A feral eyed the pot-bellied couple. "Climb as high as you can and stay there. Don't make the mistake of foraging on the lower lands."

"Don't worry," Charlie smiled, "we have enough cash to create a detour," contentedly his eyes fell upon the black sacks, "something to throw their silly minds off course."

"But…" It was Indy, "surely these hills will be the first place they search."

"Indeed," Charlie agreed, "that's why we need a diversion. One, that makes it look like all the animals have been stolen, rather than escaped."

"Stolen?" It was Purditta, her blue eyes wide as saucers, while posing at the same time, before Charlie.

"Yep...! And I know just the man."

"Who...?" It was Gigs.

"Den, of course." Charlie beamed at the black sacks then at Vermin, who was comfortably sat on them.

"How on earth is he going to steal all the animals? It was Indy. "For a start they're already out and secondly, he couldn't keep them all, if he had the space!"

"Talking of which," Vermin snuffled, "What about the giraffe? How on earth is he going to keep his head down?"

The cats chuckled. Catching on, the giraffe gave out a gaggle of his own. "If it's the difference between a cage and a cave," the giraffe gave out a second giggle, "I guess, I'll have to get used to lowering my head."

"C'mon you lot," Croft, and the cats took off. Finding their feet, the animals ran after them. Once inside the woods, they split up and took them off in different directions. Exhausted from all the excitement, Trike turned to Poo, Purditta and Charlie who was watching the woods.

"If there is nothing else, will you take me home?"

"Of course," Poo and Purditta watched him get up and began walking beside him.

"There is one thing," Charlie called to Purditta, "if you hang back a minute that is?"

"Sure…" Her silhouette was a heavenly shadow.

Relying on Den, Charlie's mind was made up.

"What's, on your mind wild one?" Oozing confidence, her words were almost flippant.

"How's your timekeeping?"

"Remarkable…" Purditta nodded while deliberately showing off her shapely figure.

"Shall I reel it all off, in one go then?" Charlie grew closer to her.

A paw cupped around her ear, Charlie whispered the details.

Vermin occasionally heard her say, "Ahha, okay, hmmm, hmm, really." She pushed her head closer to his ear, "bring it on baby."

Bouncing away, she accompanied Trike and Poo, over the slopes.

"Well, whatever you expressed," Vermin sighed, "seems to have made her happy."

"C'mon," Charlie cackled, "grab some of this cash."

Taking two sacks each, Charlie and Vermin, carried them across the land, over the hill and into the village. The cash, safely hidden in their back yard they were weary. Once inside the house, Vermin expressed a growing concern for the animals and their welfare.

"What if…?" He hesitated.

"There are no ifs or buts, it's going to, go with a big bang!" Charlie smiled, he curled up, purred and tried to calm his hopeful, mind.

Runaway Rogues

It was 3am when Gigs, Balloo and Indy returned. Animals all safe, blisters on their feet, they had never been more pleased to be home. Not long behind them, sacks thrown over their shoulders, the ferals followed. Money lobbed over the wall, they too longed for some sleep. Up at eight, Charlie took out some cash, while at the same time, contemplated the best way to approach Den. He was in mid thought when a loud whistle was heard.

Out the front, and bang on time, it was Purditta. Charlie pushed the bin bags under a bench and went to meet her. Stood beside Dens car, wearing a pink boob tube and pedal pushers, she was spring flower radiant. Sign under the window wiper, the writing was red.

"Are the rest in place?" Charlie asked. Tired, and totally thrilled to see her, he struggled with the butterflies in his belly.

"Of course, Mackison has made a special journey back to the sanctuary with the other two."

Gosh, her voice is sweet, he thought. Charlie couldn't help but stare at her. "Right, well, I'll get to it." Approaching the vehicle, he put some cash behind the newly made sign.

"Wish me luck!"

Charlie then went upstairs, climbed onto the bed and planted himself on Den's head.

"Get off!" Bolt upright, Denis brushed Charlie aside and wiped the touch from his head and hair. Too early to endure crazy cats his eyes were ablaze. Examining Charlie more closely his mood simmered.

"Cats got cash!" He blurted to Becky.

"In your dreams…!" Becky turned over and went back to sleep.

Brandishing a 500 euro, Charlie began backing up to the door where he dropped the note. Bingo! Den expressed eagerness.

"I do believe the little ragamuffin wants me to follow him" Gathering up a pair of trousers, Den punched in one leg and tripped every two seconds while putting the other in. Denis, as planned picked up the cash and paraded after him. On reaching his car he saw a 500, note stuffed under a sign. Only money in mind, he tore both the cash and note away from the window wipers.

It read. "There is more money to be had at the sanctuary." Den got in the car and started it. Charlie and Vermin leapt onto the bumper. Slippery they had to hang on to the boot handle. Sliding from side to side they were relieved to arrive at the sanctuary. Leaping down from the bumper, Den eyed Charlie and Vermin with suspicion. Sprinting, they hurried towards a white transit belonging to the sanctuary and got in it. Another sign, it had been strategically placed on the screen, under it, another note.

"What the heck!" Denis took down the money and examined the sign. On the back of the cardboard was a map.

"Enter and exceed the speed limit this is an absolute emergency. In Calpe you find more cash, just follow the map."

Nicely stolen by Mackison the keys were dangling in the ignition for him. Vermin and Charlie held their breath as they waited for Den to take the challenge. Intrigued he got in, sparked up the van and drove like the clappers to Calpe. Den pulled up a few yards from a circus. Completely bewildered, he scratched his head.

Charlie glared at Vermin, "Now here's the crucial bit."

Charlie opened the glove box and dragged out another sign that he held up for Den to read. It said, 'now pick us up and run!'

Shoving another note at Den, Charlie and Vermin hopped into his arms. Sensing a dodgy situation, Den took the cash. Running like the clappers to the nearest road he hailed a taxi cab that he instructed to take them back to the village. Den put Charlie on the back seat, Vermin he threw on the floor.

"I dunno what you've done but your one crazy little cat!"

Mission achieved, Charlie and Vermin squeaked in amusement. Back in the village car park, Denis paid the driver. Opening the door for them, Charlie and Vermin stepped out of the cab. Rather flabbergasted and still in disbelief, he glared at them scornfully. Feeling good, Charlie glanced up at the balcony, sat slumped to one side, a scotch in his wrinkly hand, Miguel sipped at it. To the right of him in a pair of sexy shorts and sunglasses, was Purditta. Charlie couldn't see through the tinted lenses, but he knew that she was staring right at him.

"All done...?" She mused.

Hooked, Charlie gave her a heart-felt smile, a moment later the thumbs up. Turning, he saw Mackison beside the bins, his usual gluttony displayed, he showed no shame as the last of the fish tail slithered down his throat. Running to greet them the ferals gave Charlie and Vermin a high five. Bewilderment displayed on Dens face, the cats broke into bouts of laughter.

"This can't be, it's ludicrous," he exclaimed out loud, "animals aren't that clever."

"Speak for yourself!" Charlie mocked.

Content with the cash acquired, but still without a clue as to how, Den followed Charlie and Vermin home.

Denis didn't try to stop Vermin from entering. Instead, he went indoors and had a count up.

That night, the ferals returned to the hills and checked that the animals were safe. It was a strange night, full of wonder and worry, neither Den, or the animals slept. The next morning, bright and early, Becky bustled towards the kitchen table.

"Look at this," she said excitedly waving a newspaper around.

"Go on, see if you can surprise me some more?" Baffled by his comment, Becky began reading.

"A local sanctuary was ransacked and robbed of all its inhabitants and income. Speculation says that it would have taken at least six men to carry out the theft. It is believed they gained entry through the back of the property and left through the front gate. Amongst the missing animals are exotic big cats, chimps, bears and a giraffe. The whereabouts of them is yet unknown. However, the ford transit belonging to the sanctuary was discovered during the early hours this morning outside an illegal circus in Calpe. Renowned for its trade of exotic species, it is believed that the animals were taken there before being relocated to other profiting places. Authorities say that it is unlikely the animals will be recovered. According to statistics, a considerable amount of money donated by the public is also missing. Due to the discovery of ill treatment within the sanctuary, it has now been closed down and an enquiry into the funding of the sanctuary opened."

Clearly content, both Trike and Poo smiled.

"Well I'll be dammed!" Denis fell into the armchair and started to explain the strange chain of events.

"If," Becky quizzed, "what you say is true, then what the hell did Charlie do with a dozen big cats and chimps? I mean for Goodness sake, a giraffe."

"Wouldn't you like to know," Stood in the doorway it was Charlie and Vermin.

Denis pulled out one of the instruction signs, "there's something about this writing but I just can't put my finger on it yet!"

"You're not telling me you think Charlie can write now?"

Denis gave her a strange look then grabbed a dictionary. He opened the pages and began reading words at random. "Siberian, sanctuary, style...."

"There's something you don't have!" Charlie sniggered.

Recognizing the snigger, Denis slammed the book shut and peered towards the kitchen door.

"Where's the cash Charlie, come on show me."

Charlie cowered away and hissed, Trike moved forward in a defensive manner.

"Look," Den simmered, "I said you were crazy, but actually you're a really clever cat! If, you have some spare cash, it could help Trike. You know get him all the care we can while we can."

"Christ," Charlie shrieked, "I gave him hundreds earlier, what does he think I am, a cat cash machine?"

"Oh, give it him," Vermin chuckled, "it's not like you haven't got it."

"I didn't say, no did I?" Charlie was fond of Trike, and for sure, would miss the big trundle bundle and his old wheel when he was gone.

"Let's bring in a bag." Charlie encouraged Vermin to follow him. Attaching Vermin's dungarees to one of the black sacks, they dragged it in and emptied it on the carpet.

"Wow," used notes around and under their feet, Denis and Becky synchronized. No time to waste, Denis undid the wheel. Scooped Trike into his arms and whisked him away to the vets.

"I just hope they can provide something," Gigs entered, "do something to prolong his life."

"Yeah, poor old Trike..." Balloo balanced his wheel against the wall.

Still in shock, Becky busied herself putting the used notes into manageable bundles while at the same time, comforting Poo.

"C'mon," Charlie struggled with words, "if we stay, we'll all be in tears."

The bins were bee hive busy with cats. "Hey, Charlie how ya doing," one of them greeted, "we've got enough cash to buy all the fish we want now."

"You're just in time," Mackison interrupted. Paws around a bottle of cat champagne, he was trying to pull the wire plug from its top.

"Where did you get that?" Charlie gasped in surprise.

"Mandy buys all sorts of stupid stuff, more money than sense."

"Not anymore," Croft crossed his arms, "we've got it all." There was a loud synchronized cackle.

"Welcome country cats to our Feral, Fiesta." Already drunk another of them cat walked towards Charlie.

There was a loud sucking sound. A second later, the pop of a cork flew into the air. "Here we go me old chums," he poured plonk into paper cups, "did alright didn't we…?"

"Didn't we just," came a sultry voice.

The eyes of many maneuvered upwards and towards the balcony. Pushing past Miguel, wearing a pair of pink trousers and matching top, was Purditta. Her butt pinching trousers exhibiting quite a view, she wriggled down the drainpipe. Reaching the bottom, she took the liberty of planting a big wet kiss on the lips of Charlie Bonker. Blushing, his cheeks puffed up like an angelic peacock, she then took hold of his paw. Charlie felt strange, almost awkward in front of the ferals but at the same time pleased. Envious and excited the cats made a loud cheering sound. Catching the attention of Miguel, he leaned over the balcony…

"Mandy," he scorned, "my pedigree Persian is down there with what appears, to be a local ragamuffin!"

Mandy smiled. "Never mind dear…"

"Never mind…! I don't want her breeding with that sort, he's a feral!"

Mandy raised her eyebrows. "Oh, do shut up dear, have you forgotten that you, was, once a peasant, don't be judgmental, it doesn't suit you!"

"Right that does it." Miguel got up, but too much alcohol in the sun had made him dizzy, forcing him to sit back down and swallow the situation.

"Besides," said Mandy, "seems quite a looker from here, quite a dish."

"I'll give you a dish." Miguel threw a saucer over the balcony towards the cats where it shattered. The cats cracked up laughing. More plonk and they raved it up. It was late afternoon when Denis and Becky returned. Spotting Charlie by the bins, Den stopped to share the news. According to the test carried out, the cancer had spread beyond control, the diagnosis, death within the week. Face gaunt and haunted, Trike stared out of the car window. Silence amongst the cats, they watched Den drive down the hill towards home.

"All we can do," Purditta put her paws together, "is make sure his every wish is met. Get him out at night, sit with him and exchange stories until…"

The cats fell silent.

And so that's exactly what they did. Night after night, Trike, the cats and Vermin, ventured to the hillside. There, stars upon them, moon shining, they examined the higher peaks with curious eyes. Once or twice they thought they saw something moving through the trees, the possibilities bringing a lot of satisfaction. It was the fourth night, when Trike asked that his wheel, be removed. Poo was silent, her feelings subdued, she knew what to expect. Words were not something that came easily, and even cheeky Charlie struggled to find anything suitable to say. They removed the wheel pretending everything was ok. Trike lay down, but, every now and then he would look up at the stars, his eyes wandering towards the forest in the distance. Despite his disability, he had participated in something worthwhile and wonderful. His last wish was to see some of the liberated animals, find out how freedom was treating them and how they were coping. On his feet Indy was gone before Trike had even finished. It was midnight when he returned, a bear and tiger either side of him.

"Trike my friend," said the bear, "If we could trade anything to give you a longer life it would be yours."

"How is life outside the sanctuary?" Trike enquired.

"Thanks to you all," the bear acknowledged everyone present, "we now know what life's really about."

"That's good." Trike closed his eyes, his spirit leaving he was gone.

The bear went to scoop him up, but Charlie said it was best to leave him. The last thing he wanted, was for Denis to be shining a torch over the hills. The bear bid them farewell and with the tiger in tow, disappeared into the tendrils of mist that had gathered upon the hills.

Upset, Denis arrived to take Trike away. Sat in his arm chair he fell asleep with him on his lap. Leaving him, Becky went to bed in tears. Tugging on every single sack, Charlie didn't stop until they were all inside the front room for when Denis woke up. A mound of money now at his disposal, Denis decided to do something constructive for all of them. Many things on his mind he went out in search of land. A plot by the river, far away from local life, he bought it without hesitation. On the land he buried Trike, many memories of him to be cherished the old liability was to become a legend, one never to be forgotten. Thoughts turning to the Ferrell's he wanted them to have somewhere better than the streets to sleep, this in mind he ordered materials and built a big out house for them. Daily, Becky put fresh milk, cushions and plenty of tasty foods inside it. Free to come and go as they pleased the cats did exactly that. To the disappointment of Miguel, Purditta visited the land more often that he cared to count...

For Trike, a damned good dog!

www.ingramcontent.com/pod-product-compliance
Lightning Source LLC
Chambersburg PA
CBHW020808130626

46554CB00006B/2332